BEAUTIFUL YETTA'S

Hanukkah Kitten

By
DANIEL
PINKWATER

Illustrated by
JILL
PINKWATER

FEIWEL AND FRIENDS
NEW YORK, NY

In the beautiful city of Brooklyn, people are happy. They work and shop, and look after children who play and go to school. There are birds, cats and dogs, squirrels and rats . . . and parrots!

Yes! There are parrots in Brooklyn.
Once pets, they now live in trees and parks.
And there is one chicken who lives with them.

Yetta, beautiful Yetta! She escaped from the
poultry market and now lives with the wild parrots.
She is brave and clever, and the parrots love her.
She is like their mother.

I have found a home in Brooklyn.
איך האָב אַ היים געפֿונען אין בראָאָקלין.
ikh hob a heym gefunen in Brooklyn.

We love this chicken!
She is like our mother.
¡Nos encanta esta gallina!
Ella es como nuestra madre.
Nos enCANta ESSta gahYEEna!
EHya ess como NWEHStra MAdray.

The parrots like to gather around her and listen to stories of her life on a chicken farm, running through the fields and eating bugs, before she came to Brooklyn.

Winter has come to Brooklyn. The trees have lost
their leaves, and the wind is cold. Yetta and the parrots
fluff their feathers and huddle together at night.

But there are seeds and pizza crusts to eat, and sometimes a bagel.
And the parrots have built a warm nest on top of a streetlight.

Mew!

On a snowy night, Yetta hears a tiny noise.

In a snowdrift, Yetta finds a tiny kitten.
It is cold. It is hungry. It is lost.

Yetta wraps her wings around the kitten.

The parrots are confused. Why is Yetta hugging a cat? Aren't cats dangerous?

Help me
take care
of it.
חעלף מיר
מיט איר.
help mir mit ir.

Beautiful Yetta and the parrots realize they do not know how to take care
of the kitten. They need an idea, but they have no idea.

Then . . . Yetta gets an idea.

We will take her to the old grandmother!

ברענגט איר צו דער אַלטע באָבען.

brengt ir tsu der alte boben.

The old grandmother is a lady the parrots know.
She puts bread crumbs on the windowsill for them.
The parrots like her.

The parrots gather around the kitten on the grandmother's doorstep.
Yetta flies to the windowsill, and taps on the glass with her beak.

Yetta asks the grandmother to go to her door.
The parrots have something for her.

"Don't go away," the grandmother tells Yetta and the parrots.
"Go to the windowsill and wait."

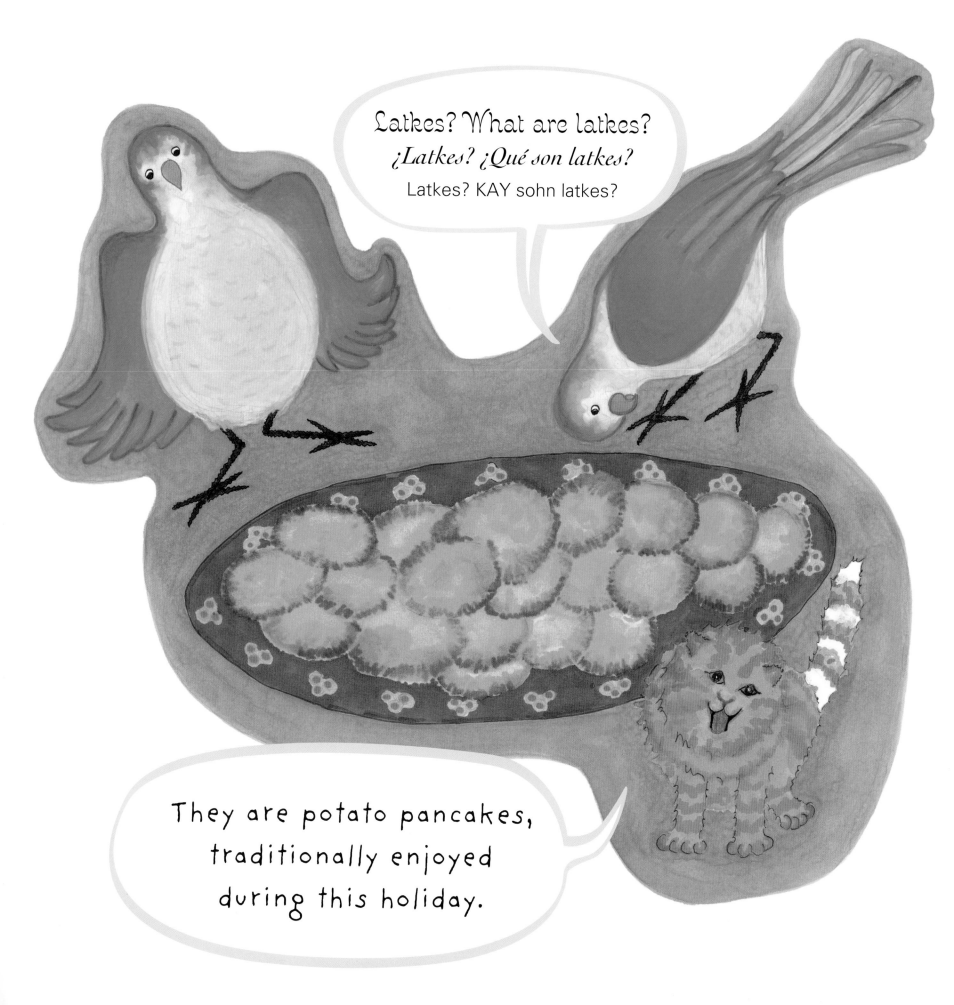

To Isabel,
my sister who taught
me about books.
—D. P.

To Phyllis,
my venerable sister
and friend.
—J. P.

A FEIWEL AND FRIENDS BOOK
An Imprint of Macmillan

Library of Congress Cataloging-in-Publication Data Available

ISBN: 978-0-312-62134-6

Yiddish translation by Yael Strom
Spanish translation by Alicia Padrón and Guillermo Casallo

The artwork was created using Prismacolor indelible markers and brush pens, and pen and ink on Bristol board.

Feiwel and Friends logo designed by Filomena Tuosto

First Edition: 2014

1 3 5 7 9 10 8 6 4 2

mackids.com

Yiddish and Hebrew use a different alphabet than English, and are written from right to left, instead of left to right (as in English). The chart to the right shows the Hebrew alphabet, written in Hebrew alphabetical order, so *Alef* is the first letter and *Tav* is the last. This alphabet is often called the "*aleph-bet*," because of its first two letters.

Hebrew letter	י	ט	ח	ז	ו	ה	ד	ג	ב	א	
Pronunciation	Y	T	Ch	Z	V	H	D	G	B/V	silent	
Letter name	Yod	Tet	Chet	Zayin	Vav	He	Dalet	Gimel	Bet	Alef	

Hebrew letter	ע	ס	ן	נ	ם	מ	ל	ך	כ	
Pronunciation	silent	S	N	N	M	M	L	Kh	K/Kh	
Letter name	Ayin	Samech	Nun	Nun	Mem	Mem	Lamed	Khaf	Kaf	

Hebrew letter	ת	ש	ר	ק	ץ	צ	ף	פ	
Pronunciation	T	Sh/S	R	Q	Ts	Ts	F	P/F	
Letter name	Tav	Shin	Resh	Qof	Tsadik	Tsadik	Feh	Peh